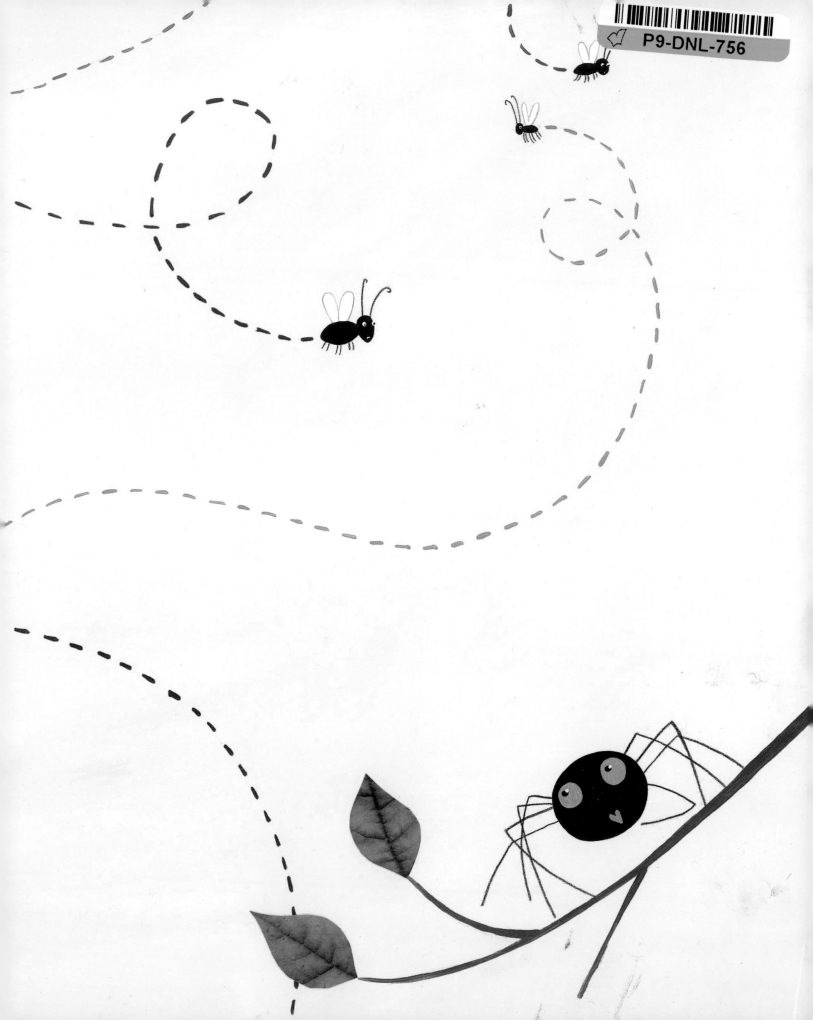

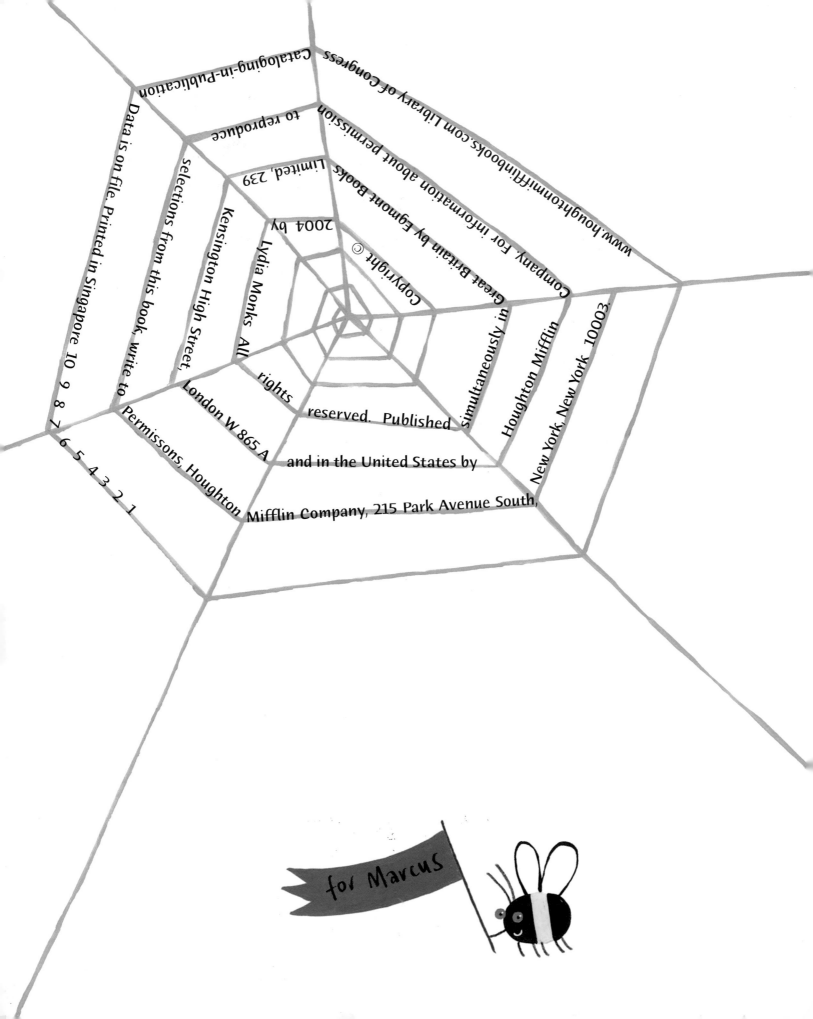

for Marcus

Aaaarrgghh! Spider!

Lydia Monks

Houghton Mifflin Company
Boston 2004

It's really lonely
being a spider.
I want to be a
family pet.

THIS
family's pet!

I know!
I'll show them what a great dancer I am.
None of their pets can dance like me!

"Look at me! Watch me dance!"

None of their pets are clean like me!

"Out

you

go!"

Oh, dear!

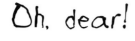

I know!
I'll show them how easy
I am to look after.

None of their
pets can feed
themselves
like I can!

"Out you go!"

It's no good.
This family will
never want me.

I'm going to go
and live all alone . . .

. . . in the backyard.

Look at me! Watch me ride!

Look at me! Watch me shop!

Look at me! Watch me swing!

I'm a real, true, proper pet!

In fact, I'm so happy with my new family,
I think I'll introduce them to all my friends . . .